10,000 MANIACS
BLIND MAN'S ZOO

Amsco Publications
New York/London/Sydney

Musical Arrangements by Frank Metis

This book Copyright © 1989 Amsco Publications,
A Division of Music Sales Corporation, New York, N.Y.

All rights reserved. No part of this book may be
reproduced in any form or by any electronic or
mechanical means including information storage
and retrieval systems, without permission in writing
from the publisher except by a reviewer who
may quote brief passages in a review.

Order No. AM 75789
International Standard Book Number: 0.8256.1214.4

Exclusive Distributors:
Music Sales Corporation
225 Park Avenue South, New York, NY 10003

Printed in the United States of America by
Vicks Lithograph and Printing Corporation

THE BIG PARADE 22

DUST BOWL 29

EAT FOR TWO 4

HATEFUL HATE 56

HEADSTRONG 48

JUBILEE 62

THE LION'S SHARE 76

PLEASE FORGIVE US 16

POISON IN THE WELL 9

TROUBLE ME 36

YOU HAPPY PUPPET 42

EAT FOR TWO

Music and Words: Natalie Merchant

Copyright © 1989 Christian Burial Music, ASCAP.
All rights reserved. Used by permission.

Fm
Eb/G
Eb
Cm
Ab
Dream child in my head is a night - mare born in a
Db/F
Db
Ab
Cm
bor - rowed bed. Now I know light - ning strikes a - gain.
Bbm7
Db
Ab
It struck me once,
Cm
Bbm7
Db
then struck me dead. My fol - ly
3fr.
4fr.

grows in-side of me. _____ I

eat for two, ___ walk for two, ___ breathe for two ___ now. ___

Eat for two, ___ walk for two, ___

breathe for two ___ now. ___

2. Well, the
3. When the

Instrumental solo

Walk for two? I'm_ stum - bl - ing._

Breathe for two? I..._ I can't breathe._

I can't breathe._

Instrumental solo

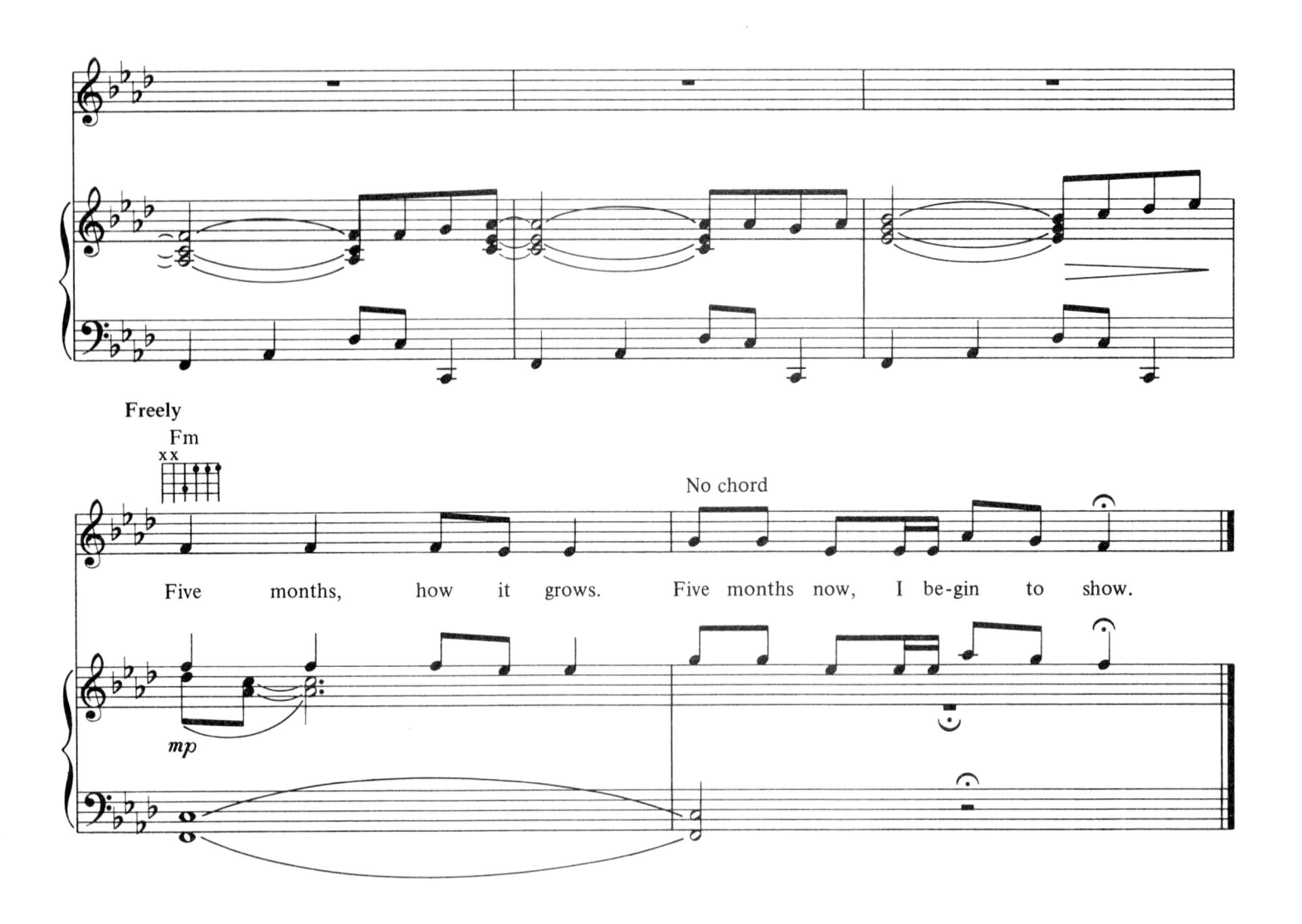

Five months, how it grows. Five months now, I be-gin to show.

Additional Lyrics

2. Well, the egg man fell down off his shelf.
   All the good king's men with all their help
   Struggled 'til the end
   For a shell they couldn't mend.

   You know where this will lead,
   To hush and rock in the nursery
   For the kicking one
   Inside of me.

   I eat for two, walk for two, breathe for two now.
   Eat for two, walk for two, breathe for two now.

3. When the boy was a boy, and a girl was a girl,
   And they found each other in a wicked world.
   Strong in some respects,
   But she couldn't stand for the way he begged

   And gave in. Pride is for men.
   Young girls should run and hide instead.
   Risk the game
   By taking dares with "yes."

   Eat for two, walk for two, breathe for two now.
   Eat for two, walk for two, breathe for two now. *(To 3rd ending)*

POISON IN THE WELL

MUSIC: DENNIS DREW
WORDS: NATALIE MERCHANT

Copyright © 1989 Christian Burial Music, ASCAP.
All rights reserved. Used by permission.

G
Gsus2/4
G
Gsus2/4
pa - per.
Call the neigh- bors.
C
G
Who's to blame
for what's go - ing on?
C
Bm
In the dark
with - out a clue,
I'm just the same
as you.
Am
G
Bm/F♯
Oh, they
tell us
there's

poi-son in__ the well,__ that some-one's been__ a bit un-ti-dy and__ there's been__ a small spill. Not a lot,__ no,__ just a drop.

1. But

there you are mis-tak-en, I know you are.

I won-der just how long

they knew our well was poi-soned, but they let us just drink on.

Oh, they tell us there's poison in the well, That someone's been a bit untidy and there's been a small spill, and all that it amounts to is a tear in a salted sea, that

someone's been a bit untidy. They'll have it cleaned up in a week. But the week is over, and now it's grown into years since I was told that I should be calm, there's nothing to fear *here.*

2. But I

They'll have it cleaned up in a week.

Additional Lyrics

2. But I drank that water for years, my wife and my children.
So tell me where to now,
If your fight for a bearable life
Can be fought and lost in your own backyard?

Oh, don't tell us there's poison in the well.
That someone's been a bit untidy,
That there's been a small spill,
And all that it amounts to is a tear in a salted sea.
That someone's been a bit untidy, *(to Coda)*

PLEASE FORGIVE US

MUSIC: ROBERT BUCK
WORDS: NATALIE MERCHANT

Moderately, with a moving beat

"Mer - cy, mer - cy," why did-n't we hear__ it?

"Mer - cy, mer - cy," why__ did we read__ it bur - ied on the

Copyright © 1989 Christian Burial Music, ASCAP.
All rights reserved. Used by permission.

17

last page of our morn-ing pa-pers?

1. The plan was draft-ed, draft-ed in se-cret.

Gun-boats met the red tide, driv-en to the rum trade for the

ar-my that they cre-a-ted. But the

bul - lets were bought by us,— it was dol - lars that paid them.—

Please for - give us,— we don't know what— was done.—

Please for - give us,— we

1.
don't know what— was done— in our name.— There'll be

2.
G
D/F♯
Domit3rd
5fr.
A
C♯m/G♯
4fr.
did - n't know
Could you ev - er for - give us? I
G
D/F♯
Domit3rd
5fr.
Eomit3rd
7fr.
don't know
how you could.
Instrumental solo
Aomit3rd
Eomit3rd
7fr.
1.
f
2.
Domit3rd
5fr.
Eomit3rd
7fr.
I know this is
no con - so - la - tion.
mf

Please forgive us, we don't know what was done. Please forgive us, we didn't know. Could you ever believe that we didn't know. Please forgive us, we

Additional Lyrics

2. There'll be more trials like this in mercenary heydays.
   When they're so apt to wrap themselves up in the stripes and stars
   And find that they are able to call themselves heroes,
   And to justify murder by their fighters for freedom.

   Please forgive us, we don't know what was done.
   Please forgive us, we didn't know. *(To 2nd ending)*

THE BIG PARADE

MUSIC: JEROME AUGUSTYNIAK
WORDS: NATALIE MERCHANT

Moderately slow, quasi march

De-troit to D.C. night train, Cap-i-tol, parts East. Lone young man take a seat.

Copyright © 1989 Christian Burial Music, ASCAP.
All rights reserved. Used by permission.

And by the rhyth-m of the rails, reading all his moth-er's mail from a cit-y boy in a jun-gle town, post-marked Sai - gon. He'll go live his moth-er's dream, join the

slow - est pa - rade he'll ev - er see. Her weight of sor - rows car - ried long and car - ried far, "Take these, Tom - my, to The Wall." It's Met - ro line to the Mall site with a tour of Jap - an - ese. He's wan - der - ing and lost un - til a Vet in worn fa - tigues takes him down to where they be - long.

D.S. al Coda

Coda

for - ty pac - es to the year that he was slain. His hand's slip - ping down The Wall for it's slick with rain.

How would life have ev-er been the same___ if this wall had carved in it one less name? But for Christ's sake, he's been dead___ o-ver twen-ty years. He leaves the let-ters ask-ing, "Who caused my moth-er's tears,__ was it

Wash - ing - ton or the Vi - et Cong?"

Slow de - lib - er - ate steps are in - volved. He

takes them a - way from the black gran - ite wall to - ward the

oth - er mon - u - ment so white and clean.

Additional Lyrics

𝄋 4. Near a soldier, an ex-Marine
   With a tattooed dagger and an eagle trembling.
   He bites his lip beside a widow breaking down.
   She takes her Purple Heart, makes a fist, strikes The Wall.

   All come to live a dream,
   To join the slowest parade they'll ever see.
   Their weight of sorrows carried far,
   All taken to The Wall.

   It's ... *(To Coda)*

DUST BOWL

Music: Robert Buck
Words: Natalie Merchant

Copyright © 1989 Christian Burial Music, ASCAP.
All rights reserved. Used by permission.

take them back,_ you know_ bet-ter than that." Dolls that talk, as-tro-nauts, T.V. games, air-planes,_ they don't un-der-stand,_ and how can I_ ex-plain? I try and try, but I can't save._ Pen-nies, nick-els, dol-lars slip_ a-way.

I've tried and tried, but I can't save.

My young-est girl has bad_ fev-er, sure.

All_ night with al-co-hol_ to cool_ and rub her

down. Ru-by, I'm tried, try and get some sleep. I'm ad-ding doc-tor's fees to rem-e-dies with the cost of three days work lost. I try and try, but I can't save. Pen-nies, nick-els,

dol-lars slip a-way. I've tried and tried, but I can't save. The hole in my pock-et-book is grow - ing. There's a new wind blow-ing, they say, it's gon-na be a cold, cold one. So brace your-selves,_ my dar - lings,_ it won't bring an-y-thing much our way_ but more_____ dust bowl days. I played a days. card in this week's game._ Took the first

last time ritard.

and the last let-ters in three of their names._

This_ lot-ter-y's_ been build-ing up for weeks._

_ I could be luck-y me with the five mil-lion prize, tears of

dis- be- lief_ spill-ing out of my eyes._ I try and

D.S. al Fine

TROUBLE ME

MUSIC: DENNIS DREW
WORDS: NATALIE MERCHANT

*Copyright © 1989 Christian Burial Music, ASCAP.
All rights reserved. Used by permission.*

on the days when you _____ feel spent. _____
when your si - lence is _____ my great - est fear? _____

Why let your shoul - ders bend _____ un - der - neath _____ this bur -
den when _____ my back is stur - dy and strong? _____

Trou - ble me. _____ Speak to me,
Speak to me. _____ Let me

don't mis-lead__ me, the calm I feel means a storm is swell-ing.__
have a look__ in - side these eyes while I'm learn - ing.__

__ Speak to me, there's no tell - ing where it starts or how it ends.__
__ Let me, please don't hide__ them just be - cause of tears.__

1. 2.

Let me send you

off to sleep__ with a, "There, there, now stop your turn-ing and toss - ing."__

Let me, let me know where the hurt is and how to heal.

Spare, spare me?

Don't spare me anything troubling.

Trou-ble me, dis-turb me with all your cares and your wor-ries. Speak to me and let our words build a shel-ter from the storm. Let me, and last-ly, let me know what I can mend.

There's more, hon-est-ly, than my sweet friend, you can see. Trust is what I'm of-fer-ing if you trou-ble me.

YOU HAPPY PUPPET

MUSIC: ROBERT BUCK
WORDS: NATALIE MERCHANT

Moderate disco beat

How did they teach you to be just a hap-py pup-pet danc-ing on a string?

How did you learn ev-ery-thing that
How do you man-age to live in-

Copyright © 1989 Christian Burial Music, ASCAP.
All rights reserved. Used by permission.

43

comes a - long with slav - ish fun - ner - y?
side this ti - ny stage you can't leave?

Tell me some-thing, if the world is so in-sane,

is it mak-ing you sane a - gain to let an - oth - er

man tug at the thread that pulls up your nod-ding head?

44

head? How did they teach you to be just a happy puppet dancing on a string? How do you manage to speak, your mouth a frozen grin? A dull-ard strung on the wire. _____ When the mas-ter's gone, you hang there with your eyes and your limbs so life-less. Tell me some-thing, if the world is so in-sane, is it mak-ing you sane a-gain to let an-oth-er

47

man tug at the thread that pulls up your emp-ty wood-en head? Your hol-lowed head, your mar-ble eyes, your wood-en hands and your met-al jaw pins all__ wait in lim-bo for the man who knows how to move you this way.

HEADSTRONG

Music and Words: Natalie Merchant

E♭ B♭ F
ten, to your voice of rea - son try - ing to change my
mind. I mind my feel - ings and not your words.
E♭
Did - n't you no - tice, I'm so head - strong
B♭ F
e - ven when I know I'm wrong.

Take this to your heart_ and in - to your head_ now.

Be - fore_ you waste_ your time,_ call a truce_ _ and call_ a draw._

What's the use_ in map - ping your views_ out in or - der - ly from,_

— when it does nothing but confuse — and anger me more. — I mind my feelings and not your words. — Didn't you notice, I'm so headstrong. You're talking to a deaf — stone wall. —

Take this to your heart and in-to your head now, the old wives' tale is true, I'll re-peat it. All is fair in love and war, that's how the fa-mous say-ing goes.

O - pen up your eyes.___ See me for what I am:___

F
C
F
cast in i - ron. I won't
Bb
C
Bb
break and I won't bend. Oh, take this to your heart
Dm/A
Gm
and in - to your head now, the
Bb
Dm/A
Gm
old wives' tale is true, I'll re - peat it.

All is fair in love and war, that's how the famous saying goes.

2. If I

Lis-ten, I think they were talk-ing to you.

poco rit.

Additional Lyrics

2. If I told you we were out to sea in a bottomless boat,
   You'd try anything to save us,
   You'd try anything to keep us afloat.

   And if we were living in a house afire,
   I don't believe that you could rush out and escape it,
   And not rescue me.

   Take this to your your heart and into your head now,
   The old wives' tale is true, I'll repeat it.
   All is fair in love and war, that's how the famous saying goes. *(to Coda)*

HATEFUL HATE

Music and Words: Natalie Merchant

(optional: Ah. _____)

1. In the

dark night a gi-ant slum-bered, un-touched for cen-tu-ries, 'til a-wak-ened by a white man's cry: "This is the E-den I was to find." There were lands to be chart-ed and to be claimed for a crown, When a he - ro was made by the length he could stay in this dan - ger - ous land of

hate - ful hate.
(3. Such a hate - ful hate).

Cu - ri - os - i - ty filled the heads of these,

There was an up - per room they had to see. Cu - ri - os - i - ty killed the best of these for a he-ro's home-town wel-com-ing.

melody

Still they moved on and on, and ... on and on, and ...

D.S. al Coda

Coda

Such a hate-ful hate.

60

Additional Lyrics

2. Who came building missions? Unswerving men of the cloth
   Who gave their lives in numbers untold
   So that black sheep entered the fold.
   Captured like human livestock, destined for slavery.
   Naked, walked to the shore
   Where great ships moored for the hellbound journies.
   Bought and sold with a hateful hate.

   Curiosity filled the breasts of these with some strange ecstacy.
   Curiosity killed the best of these by robbing their lives of dignity.
   Still they moved on and on, and ...

3. Calling men of adventure for a jungle bush safari.
   Come conquer the beast, his claws and teeth.
   See death in his eyes to know you're alive.
   European homesteads grew up in colonies
   With civilized plans for wild hinterlands.
   Their guns and their God willing.
   Such a hateful hate. *(to Coda)*

JUBILEE

Music and Words: Natalie Merchant

Freely

Moderately, a tempo, flowingly
Verse 1

He fills the flower vases, trims the candle bases, takes small change from the poor box.

Copyright © 1989 Christian Burial Music, ASCAP.
All rights reserved. Used by permission.

Lyrics:
Tyler has the key. He takes nail and hammer to take up the banner of felt scraps glued together reading, "Jesus Lives In Me." Alone in the

night, he mocks the words of the preach-er, "God is feel-ing your ev-ery pain."

Verse 2

Re-pair the Christ-mas sta-ble, re-store the plas-ter an-gel. Her lips be-gin to crum-ble and her robes_ be-gin to peel._ For Bi-ble stud-y in the church base-ment, hear chil-dren_ Gos-pel cit-ing Mat-thew sev-en-teen fif-teen.* A-lone in the

*Matthew 17 : 15 Lord have mercy on my son for he is a lunatick, and sore vexed: for oftimes he falleth into the fire and oftimes into the water.

night, he mocks the arms of___ the preach - er raised to the ceil - ing, "Tell God your pain."

Verse 3

To him__ the world's_ de - filed.___ In Lot__ he sees a like - ness there. He swears his

67

Sodom will burn down. Near Sacred Blood there's a dance hall where Tyler Glen saw a black girl and a white boy kissing shamelessly. Black hands on white shoul-ders, White hands on black shoul-ders, danc-ing, and you know what's more.

Verse 4

He's God's mad dis-ci-ple, a right-eous ti-tle for The Word he heard he so mis-un-der-stood. Though sim-ple-mind-ed, a crip-pled man, to know this man is to fear this man. To shake when, to shake when, to shake when he comes. Was-n't it

God that let__ Pu - ri - tans__ in Sa - lem do what they did to the un - faith - ful.

Instrumental solo

Verse 5

Boys__ at the Ju - bi - lee__ slow - ly sink__ in - to brown - bag__ whis - key drink - ing and reel - ing on their feet.

Girls at the Jubilee in low-cut dresses yield to rough caresses and the manhandling. Black hands on white shoulders, White hands on black shoulders, dancing, and you know what's more.

mf sempre marcato al fine

Through the tall blades of grass he heads for the Ju-bi-lee, With a buck-et in his right hand full of rags soaked in gas-o-line.

74

He lifts the shingles in the dark and slips the rags there underneath. He strikes a matchstick on the box side and watches the rags ignite. He climbs the bell tower of the Sacred Blood to watch the flames—

rising high - er toward the trees.

Si - rens wail -

- ing now toward the scene.

THE LION'S SHARE

MUSIC: NATALIE MERCHANT/DENNIS DREW
WORDS: NATALIE MERCHANT

Moderately, with a beat

Can I be unhappy? Look at what I see: A beast in furs and crowned in luxury. He's a wealthy man in the poorest land, a self-

Copyright © 1989 Christian Burial Music, ASCAP.
All rights reserved. Used by permission.

ap-point-ed king. And there's no com-plain-ing while he's reign-ing. The lambs are bare of fleece and cold. The li-on has sto-len, that I'm told. There must be some crea-ture might-y as you are. The lambs go hun-gry, not fair.— The big-gest por-tion is the li-on's share.— There must be some crea-ture might-y as you are.—

To Coda

Can I— be un-hap-py? Lis-ten and— a-gree,— No words can shame— him or tame— him. The

D.S. al Coda

Coda
Em D A/C♯
As you are.
Bm Em A D F♯m/C♯
Ra - zor claws in vel - vet paws, you dunce in your guard - ed home 'Til a
Bm Em G A
strong - er beast will call on you and pounce up - on your throne.
D F♯m G D
Do we pay? Dear - ly! For the li - on takes so greed - i - ly and

he knows__ that what he's tak - en, _____ it is ours.__ That's how the wealth's di - vid -

ed. A - mong the lambs and king of the beasts,__

__ It is so one - sid - ed. Un - til the

lamb is king of the beasts,_ we live so one - sid - ed.

poco rit.